The Rich Tapestry of a Tangled Life

Jenny Telfer Chaplin

Jenny Telfer Chaplin

Published by Kinnon Enterprises Ottawa

ISBN: 978-0-9698825-5-8

PART ONE

ONE

Vera Kilgour looked up from contemplation of the supper cloth she had been instructed to embroider to see her mother enter the room, bringing with her a draught of damp, cold air from the hallway beyond. A sour look was closely followed by the words: "You haven't got very far with it I see. Honestly, Verity at this rate, you'll be lucky to have as much as a crochet-edged guest hand towel ready for your bottom drawer, far less a comprehensive and essential stock of household linen."

Despite the ready reply which sprang to her lips Vera kept her silence, knowing full well that when her mother was addressing her by her Sunday name, then all was not well. As she watched in sullen silence her mother unfastened the fur tippet from around her neck, smoothed back her bun of tightly-coiled hair and finally settled herself comfortably in the fireside Granny-chair.

"Verity. Perhaps you did not hear me ... I said you do not seem to have much to show for your afternoon's work."

Vera puffed out her cheeks in silent protest. But from the look on her mother's face, this mute insubordination served only to add fuel to her mother's anger.

"Listen to me, my girl, and listen well, this entire afternoon has been a complete and utter waste of time. First of all you get yourself into such it disreputable state with weeping that you were unfit to be seen in polite society and now it seems that you have scarcely plied your needle, despite my strict, I repeat my strict orders to finish your work on that supper cloth."

As her mother stopped speaking, Vera looked up. "But, Mother, I told you right from the start, I did not want go out with you to Mister Cranston's new tearoom."

Her mother rose to her feet. "You will tell me nothing, my fine young lady. And as to what you might or might not want, that is absolutely no concern of mine. In fact you would do well to remember the words of the Bible .... honour thy Father and thy Mother. Think on that, my dear girl before I recount this day's pathetic and time-wasting events to your dear father when he gets home from the print-shop." On the point of yet again puffing out her cheeks in exasperation and annoyance, Vera suddenly thought better of the pointless and if she were being honest, such a childish exercise.

Instead, in trying to reason with her mother she said: "But please listen to me, Mother, why on earth should it be so important that I must be seen with you at that tearoom? I'm sure there are plenty of other expensively dressed, socially ambitious mothers already there with a coterie of spinster daughters who've been unwillingly dragged along without your having to add me to the list."

Her mother looked down at her as if her only child had suddenly been deprived of all reason.

"Verity, surely that is the whole point of the carefully-planned strategy. You see, it is only the very best people, the cream of Glasgow society, who take afternoon tea there. We go to Mister Stuart Cranston's tearoom to see and to be seen. And once there, invitations are given out to respectable house-parties, visiting cards are exchanged in the process and marriageable-age daughters are thus launched with all decorum into the best social circles and ..."

Vera could feel her eyes widen in amazement. "What you have just described is nothing more or less than a cattle-market. And, Mother, marriageable-age or not, I for one will have nothing whatsoever to do with it."

Her mother's face darkened. "You, my girl will do as I say. And right now I'm saying finish your work on that embroidery and quick about it, before I report your latest misdemeanours to your father when he gets home."

Mrs Kilgour rose and turned to leave the room, but not before delivering her parting shot:

"And apple of your father's eye or not, it's high time he learned that there is such a thing as a bad apple."

As the words echoed, Vera kicked the pouffe at her feet.

TWO

Scarcely was her mother out of the room than Vera feeling that she was beyond tears, but at the same time burning with an inner rage, stabbed the threaded needle into the half-worked leaves of ornate trailing ivy in the centre of the hated cloth. Having inadvertently pierced her forefinger in the process and left a smear of blood on the cloth she swore as mightily as any shovel-wielding navvy. To match the power of her words, she next rolled the creative masterpiece into a ball and with every vestige of her energy she tossed the hated object from her, aiming it at the furthest corner of the drawing room. Just as the discarded cloth was sailing meteor-like through the air, the door opened and as the maid entered, she came within an ace of having the projectile land on her head. Patting and straightening her maid's starched cap, Bennet looked up and said: "It's certainly raining cats-n-dugs ootside in the street, but Ah didnae ken it was comin doon tablecloths here inside the hoose."

Stubbornly refusing to give birth to the bubbling laughter which involuntarily rose to her throat, Vera kept her lips tightly pressed together, assuming what she hoped was a haughty demeanour.

Vera's mother again entered the room. As they stared in silence at each other, from the angry flush on her cheeks and the beetled brow, it was at once clear that all was not well in the world of Mrs Harold Kilgour of The Grange, Number Nine, Belmont Terrace.

"Ah, there you are, Bennet. I would have expected you to be at work in the kitchen at this hour, instead of idling around here in the drawing room wasting time in pointless chatter with Miss Verity."

With great deliberation, Bennet lifted the crumpled heap of the discarded tablecloth, smoothed it out with loving hands, and folded it neatly.

"My, my, Mistress Kilgour, so it's the bairn's Sunday' name we're dealing in today, is it? What latest mischief has my poor wee Vera been up to now?"

Vera's mother, abandoning all ladylike pretensions stamped her foot in annoyance.

"For goodness sake, Bennet, how many times have I told you ... Miss Verity is no longer a bairn, as you so persistently call her. Far from being the mischievous little girl of your fond memory, she is now rather more of a decidedly thrawn and difficult seventeen-year-old woman. And I tell you this, that pert madam could cause an uproar in an empty house." Bennet turned to go, but not before with a cheeky wink at Vera, saying: "Ah'll see if I can match up the embroidery threads you require, Vera lass. And while Ah'm at it, Ah'll give the cloth a wee bit flourish with a hot iron. Your precious handiwork seems to have got a wee bit crushed when it fell down onto the floor."

Having given not an inch to her stony-faced employer, Bennet left the room with Vera's mother hot on her heels.

Vera smiled alone with her thoughts, Good old 'Busy Bennet' it would take a really strong madam to get the better of her.

THREE

The evening meal in the Kilgour household that evening was decidedly fraught with tension when Vera's mother yet again went on about her grown daughter's lack of social graces. Vera's father snapped: "Mother. Will you leave that topic? I am well aware of every minute and tedious detail, of this afternoon's supposed high drama. God knows, you've told me often enough ever since I stepped foot inside the door this evening."

Vera mentally hugged herself with delight. Not only did it prove yet again that as Daddy's wee girl she had her beloved Papa on her side. But even better, she knew her mother absolutely loathed being addressed as Mother. With more than a touch of asperity in her voice, Mrs Kilgour said: "Harold, how often must I remind you not to address me as Mother? For my sins, nothing can ever change the fact that, yes, I am Verity's mother, but I am most certainly not your mother."

Her husband sighed and deliberately changing the subject said: "Things are busier than ever now that I've taken upon myself to print our local newspaper, a real stroke of genius that, even if I do say it myself. What with circulation soaring, ever-increasing annual subscriptions from homesick Scots around the globe and the advertising revenue all looking very healthy, business is doing very well, thank you."

Vera's mother now clearly bored, smiled sweetly. "That's splendid, dear. just splendid."

As time went on and more and more of Vera's friends attended the requisite socially acceptable tea-dansant, soirees and house parties; faster and more furious became the race to capture a husband and set out on the sea of matrimony. As the number of her single girlfriends diminished, by contrast even greater and more frequent became the bitter rows between Vera and her mother. This was brought to a head when after one particularly upsetting confrontation, her mother said: "At this rate, Verity, all the eligible young men will have gone and all that will remain to you are a few sad and lonely widowers, all of whom are looking for a young wife to be their nursemaid in their fast-approaching old age. Is that what you want? For heaven's sake, girl, before your looks fade, or before you've been so long on the shelf that people begin to wonder as to the reason why. By then not one man will be at all interested in claiming you as his bride."

Verity sighed. "Mother, must we really go through this pantomime every single time that one of my friends gets to the altar? Can't we leave the subject for once? By the way you have forgotten to mention one other possibility, I could remain a Spinster of the Parish for ever."

Her mother nodded. "If that's your proposed path in life, then yes, in that case, you could be a comfort to your father and me in our old age."

Scarcely had her mother finished speaking than Vera had a mental image of an entire lifetime of bitter, angry rows with her mother. In that moment, she decided, Perhaps a husband, preferably a rich husband, might after all be the answer to save her from the fate of everlasting arguments with her mother, and all leading towards the day when she would be a skivvying nursemaid to her parents. No, my girl, not much of a prospect that, now is it? Surely there must be at least one eligible, not entirely decrepit man left for me somewhere in this City?

The June wedding of Verity Kilgour and Bob Drummond, a leading banker in the city, was attended by the cream of Glasgow society and as if to order, the sun shone from a cloudless sky. And now as Vera sat by a roaring fire on the darkest and longest of winter days, she could not help but think that the summer pageant of tea parties, soirees, mounds of expensive wedding gifts, a visiting cast of exclusive dressmakers had been nothing other than a figment of her vivid imagination. She was still deep in thought when she became aware that her husband had come into the room and in his usual authoritative tones was speaking to her. Looking up from an intensive study of her fingernails, Vera was in time to be the recipient of a husbandly peck on the cheek.

"I see you've come to a halt on the knitting-front then, dear."

At these words, Vera could feel herself tense with annoyance as she thought, Honestly, is there no end to this? First of all my mother harping on for years about my sewing a pile of utterly useless table-linen and now my husband keeping a check on my progress with matinee-jackets. So much for the promised joys of marriage.

When it became clear that no reply was forthcoming Bob shrugged his shoulders, sat down in the master's chair, then said: "I saw your father today. He was in at the bank on a matter of business."

Vera raised her head. "Oh, really. And how was he looking? Well, I hope?"

Bob laughed. "Now that he's got his only daughter safely off his hands, I'd say he looks ten years younger."

At these words, determined to give as good as she got, Vera said: "From that I gather you mean now that he's off-loaded me on to you, you're no longer an eligible man-about-town widower, and now you're the one stuck with me."

Bob stared at her, as if mentally deciding what his response should be. Then with a mirthless laugh, he said: "Couldn't have phrased it better myself. And as you so rightly say, I'm no longer a widower, so here's what I'd suggest ..."

As Vera waited to hear what might be coming, already she was dreading the outcome and wondered how best she could make her escape. She well knew that she had already overplayed her hand recently with the ritual wifely excuse of, 'I've got a headache'.

When Bob again spoke, his next words left her in no doubt as to his imminent intentions. Removing the unfinished matinee jacket from where it still lay crumpled on her lap, he said: "Since knitting garments for the coming child is apparently of little or no interest to you, Verity, I can think of other wifely pursuits. So, upstairs with you, prepare yourself and I'll join you shortly for an hour or so before dinner."

Her husband's tone of voice made it clear that far from being a polite invitation, what he had just issued was a command, an order to fulfil her matrimonial obligations. As she made her way out of the drawing room, the thought came to Vera, Just a good job that Bob has plenty of money and can keep me in comfort and buy me nice things, otherwise my life with him would be unbearable, a living hell.

FOUR

As Vera looked down at her bulging belly, the thought came to her, So much for having a trousseau of beautiful clothes. In two years of marriage all I've been able to wear has been voluminous sack like garments. Honestly I'm nothing but a baby-machine. When in God's name does my life start?

As Bennet came into the room with baby Jamie in her arms, she said: "Cheer up, Vera. Here's a wee fella in need of a cuddle from his Mammy."

Vera raised her eyes to heaven. "You know, Bennet, with your everlasting cheerfulness, there's times you really do depress me beyond belief and I wish to God you'd stayed in my dear mother's employ, rather than dogging my footsteps."

Bennet handing over the baby, grinned. "Aye, so Madam's in one of her moods again, is she? Just wait 'til the new baby arrives. Ah shouldnae think there would be any living with you then."

Later that same day with wee Jamie asleep in the nursery, her husband hard at work at his Bank in the City and Bennet, for once, nowhere to be seen, Vera heaved a sigh of relief. No sooner had she mouthed, like a heartfelt prayer the words, peace, perfect peace, than, as if it had been an incantation to tempt the Fates, the door opened to admit her mother and her mother-in-law.

The latter spoke first. "We peeped in earlier, dear, but I rather think you had dozed off. Quite natural, of course, in your interesting condition."

Vera frowned and thought, It may be interesting to you dear Mother-in-law, now that you are safely past the age of childbearing, but personally I'm just bloody bored with the whole rotten business. Interesting condition, be damned.

As Vera opened her mouth to speak, her mother doubtless having observed the warning signs of one of her daughter's habitual dark moods, at once rushed in: "We've just been upstairs to see wee Jamie. Like a little golden-haired angel, isn't he, Mathilda?" As the two women twittered on about their beautiful grandson, leaving Vera to her own dark thoughts, Bennet appeared with the tea trolley. The ritual of afternoon tea having been conducted with due decorum, the three women chatted idly about what the elder Mrs. Drummond coyly referred to as the latest matches, hatches and dispatches.

Then laying a beringed hand on Vera's arm, she said: "You know dear. I confess ... and your mother is aware of this ... but I had my doubts when Bob married you, such a chit of a girl compared to his own mature years ... but look how well it has all turned out. Already you've given me one lovely grandchild and now with another wee one on the way, I just could not be any happier."

Vera's mother nodded. "I think you speak for all of us, Mathilda. And of course, let us not forget how delighted Harold and I are with our fine successful son-in-law. The word in the City is that Bob's bank is going from strength to strength ... doing us all a power of good."

Determined not to play her expected part in this orgy of self-congratulation, Vera merely smiled sweetly, at the same time as thinking, So starts another fun afternoon in bloody, stuck-up Grosvenor Terrace.

FIVE

Despite the midwife's best efforts and her repeated exhortations to Vera to 'Push, push, just another wee push', in the end the perfectly-formed baby girl was stillborn. As Vera sat reflecting on what a senseless waste it had all been with absolutely no end-result, she suddenly smiled with the realisation that the doctors had now issued an ultimatum – a strict injunction that there should be no more babies.

How was it that Doctor Nairn had put it? "Yes, your wife is still a young woman, but in her delicate state of health, she just could not stand up to the physical effort, far less the mental anxiety of any further such bitter disappointments."

When Bob had further questioned the old doctor, the latter taking refuge behind his knowledge of the family history, said: "You forget, Mr Drummond, sir, that I have been Verity's medical practitioner since she was a little girl in ringlets and I don't believe I am breaking any patient confidentiality when I tell you that she has always been rather highly-strung. No, I am utterly convinced, any further confinements would be absolutely detrimental to her physical and above all to her mental wellbeing." And having delivered himself of this homily, the good doctor collected his consultation fee, said his goodbyes and left the Drummond family in turmoil.

Vera was secretly beside herself with glee, as she thought, Hallelujah, I'm free, I'm free. No more of that degrading business of the hour or two of marital so-called relaxation before dinner. It's over. No more wearing unsightly smocks and waddling around like a baby elephant, no more messy miscarriages. At last I can be myself. How in God's name, can so many women keep their sanity and bear a child for every twelve-months of marriage? It astounds and appals me.

Her husband's voice broke into her thoughts:

"Well now, we certainly did not expect that, did we, my dear? Of course, we're lucky to have Jamie, a fine wee lad, but I had hoped your being so young and as far as I was aware apparently healthy ... one of the reasons I married you, if I'm being honest ... my hope was that in time we'd have a houseful of bairns and at least three or four sons to follow me into the Bank." Vera stared in disbelief at her husband, amazed that they could each have such diversely opposed aims and ambitions as to how their wedded life together might have turned out.

She bit back the words which sprang to her lips and instead muttered: "We all know what the Bard said about the best-laid schemes, don't we?"

SIX

October 1878

Verity and her mother having seen Jamie tucked into his cot for the night were chatting together in the drawing room.

"You know, Verity, I must say how surprised and pleased I am at the way in which you have so graciously accepted your now barren state."

Vera felt the hot colour rush to her cheeks. "Really, Mother do we have to discuss this yet again? I have to say that I find the whole business really very embarrassing, if you must know. Perhaps it might have been better in the past if instead of berating me about my lack of social graces and training me in the finer aspects of embroidery, tatting and crochet, you had told me rather more of the facts of life, pertaining to the marriage-bed before pushing me at breakneck speed into the arms of dear Papa's Bank Manager."

Her mother drew in a horrified gasp. "Verity, I refuse to listen to such talk. It is not seemly. The facts of life; the marriage-bed indeed. That's something never discussed in polite society. And the Bank Manager you talk about ... he is now your devoted husband, he looks after you well, lavishes gowns, jewellery, expensive furs. Although, how the dear man stands your moods, your tantrums, your ill-temper, I just cannot understand."

In the silence which followed as the two women sat alone with their inner thoughts, they were aware of the sound of raised voices issuing from Bob's study across the hallway. Her father's voice, angrier than she had ever heard it in her entire life, shouted out: "For God's sake, man, it was you, you yourself who recommended those shares. And now you're telling me they're worthless, not worth the paper they're written on. I just don't believe this. My entire fortune, every penny I've earned over the years, every single farthing, is tied up in them."

Bob's voice came across as a rather conciliatory monotone. Mrs Kilgour and her daughter gazed open-mouthed at each other, too aghast by what they had just heard even to speak a single word, far less voice an opinion.

They heard the study door open then slam violently shut.

Next moment, a beetroot-red-faced Mr Kilgour staggered into the drawing room. Like an old done man, he collapsed into the nearest chair, put his head in his hands and wept with such force that his whole body seemed wracked with the raw emotion. Vera had never before seen any grown man crying, far less her stalwart, hard-headed businessman father. The whole scene was so utterly shocking to her that she felt as though her limbs were frozen into immobility and not only action of any kind but also any meaningful words were totally beyond her. One glance at her mother showed that she too was in a state of shock. As still they sat lifeless, the noise and utter hopelessness of her father's weeping grew in volume. Just then an ashen-faced Bob came into the room and astounding though it was, it was apparent from the look of him that he too had been crying.

This galvanised Vera into action and drawing her husband to a chair, she put a hand on his arm. "Bob. Mother and I ... we heard something of the shouted discussion from your study. What in the name of God, please tell us, what precisely is going on?"

Her husband shrank away from her comforting hand, looked deeply into her eyes and said: "The whole of Glasgow will know tomorrow, my Bank, the Sillarmore, my Bank is ruined. It can no longer function."

A heavy silence greeted this austere announcement, then Mrs Kilgour said: "Bob, what nonsense is this? Surely there must be some mistake?"

At these words from his wife, Vera's father lifted his tearstained face. "Oh, aye, there's a mistake all right, The mistake is that we ever listened to her Bank Manager husband and invested our entire life savings in the Sillarmore

Bank. We should have known it was all too good to last. Such wonderful interest and no problems, too good to last forever. Oh, dear God in heaven, Mother, we are ruined, utterly penniless, bankrupt, call it what you want, but as of this hellish day, we are paupers, and I say the word advisedly."

Bob heaved a deep sigh. "Yes, it's true, Mrs Kilgour, and not only for you, but also for every other single investor. Your money, their money, everybody's money has gone. And when the word gets out tomorrow, there's going to be a great many desperately unhappy people in Glasgow." He turned to face Vera. "A word to you, dear wife, you must stay close to home tomorrow, do not venture out into the streets and make sure that Bennet keeps a tight hold on wee Jamie. Once the fall of the Bank is common knowledge, there are ugly times ahead."

SEVEN

As Vera's parents took their leave and as Vera waved them on their way, she was at once acutely aware of just how very much her mother and father had aged visibly and so suddenly after the stark, totally unexpected announcement.

She was still reflecting on this when Bennet turned to her and said: "Are your folks no feeling too good, Vera? They seem a bit doon in the dumps tae me, no like their usual high spirits after a wee visit tae see the bairn."

Vera turned unseeing eyes on the family retainer and almost of their own volition, words sprang to her lips. "They've had a bit of bad news, no point in my trying to hide it, especially since the whole of Glasgow will be similarly affected by this time tomorrow."

Bennet turned with a questioning look. "Oh and what way's that?"

Vera sighed, wishing that the matter could have been left there. In an effort to minimise discussion, Vera waved her hand dismissively and said: "Nothing for you to worry about, Bennet ... it's all to do with some banking matters, stocks and shares, complicated financial details like that and I'm sure of no possible interest whatever to the likes of you."

A stunned silence greeted this decidedly condescending appraisal and it was a moment or two before Bennet, hands on hips as if ready to do battle, said: "The likes of me. Hmph, that's good Ah must say. For your information, ma lass, Ah'll have ye know this ... whatever you may think, my money's every bit as precious as any fancy stocks and shares belonging to those and such as those. What Ah suppose ye'd call my betters."

Vera was about to speak but Bennet had not yet finished. "It's a real pity your parents hadnae just played safe and put their money into a jacose wee savings account such as Ah've been paying into for years in your husband's bank." Vera's eyes widened but ignoring this, Bennet went on: "Aye, safer than houses that and like your husband once telt me, better than keeping my money in a shortbread tin under my bed. Call me daft if ye like, but even the very name of Sillarmore makes me feel safe, secure and able to sleep nights knowing that I'll aye get more money back, what with the interest, than Ah ever deposit. Aye, Sillarmore's the bank for me."

As Vera's eyes widened even more, she put a hand to her mouth to stem the rising tide of horror and utter amazement.

Seeing this reaction, Bennet tapped the side of her nose, in an expression of secrecy. "Nae need tae look sae dumfoonert that the likes of me

... as ye put it ... that the likes of me has a penny or two tae my name. Ye see, Ah've aye been careful with my wages and between that and a wee pile of money my auld Auntie Aggie left me, my bank book's lookin real healthy these days."

Unable to contain herself a moment longer, Vera gasped. "But Bennet, you don't understand ..." Bennet nodded. "Oh fine weel Ah understand ... by the time wee Jamie's going to the school, Ah'll be able tae retire in comfort, buy masell a wee but-n-ben in Millport. Then it's the Cosy Corner for me and nae mair work."

Vera laid a hand on the other woman's arm and struggled to find the words. "Listen, I'm sorry, but it's the Sillarmore Bank we're talking about. It has failed; gone to the wall, call it whatever you like, but it has ceased trading, gone down and taken all its investors and their money with it."

Scarcely were the words spoken than Bennet let out a bloodcurdling scream and fell in a dead-faint at Vera's feet.

EIGHT

When morning came, Vera awoke to the realisation that as of now her life and that of her family had changed forever.

Quite apart from the financial debacle ... and God alone knows what's still to come in the wake of all that ... thought Vera, but for almost the first time in my life here I am without the help of my dear old Busy Bennet. All right, so her fussing often annoyed me, but even so, she did cushion me in my life in so many ways.

As this line of thought took hold, it progressed to the point where, yet again, Vera was mentally reliving the horror of Bennet's collapse and subsequent removal to the Infirmary.

What was it the young doctor had said?

For some reason, he had assumed that his patient was Verity's Granny when he opined: "I am sorry to say that your grandmother has had what appears to be a massive heart-attack. And while she may make a gradual recovery, her gadding about, carefree lifestyle, knitting, crocheting and above all baby-minding days are over. She will be a changed woman."

As Vera thought back over the events of the previous evening it dawned on her that like Bennet, her own mother too was suddenly an old, dispirited woman.

Perhaps I should go round and see her this morning? That's what I'll do, I'll take wee Jamie, that should cheer her up.

But didn't Bob tell me to stay close to home today for safety's sake? She bit at her lower lip in a bout of indecision, then her face cleared. Uch to hell with obeying orders. Bob's already at the Bank; Bennet's safely in hospital; my mother's at home. So I'll damn well please myself. Anyway, what possible harm can come to us?

As Vera and her son made their way along Great Western Road, if anything the streets were quieter than usual and Vera congratulated herself in having acted on her own initiative, rather than staying at home, cowering in fear and trembling of the unknown.

NINE

Vera was within yards of her parent's home and already looking forward to a welcoming cup of tea when a door further down Belmont Terrace, was thrown open and amidst a great deal of noise and angry shouting, a wild-eyed man catapulted down the steps and on to the pavement.

Close on his heels, a distraught woman was screaming: "Hamish, I beg of you. It's only money. Not worth risking your life for."

The man raised his right arm and yelled back. "It's not my life you should be worried about. I'll shoot the first bastard bank director that I come across. And don't forget, I know who they are. Shoot the bastards so I will."

At that moment Vera to her horror saw that the man was brandishing aloft a rifle. For all of a second frozen in time, Vera was rooted to the spot. Then survival instinct to the fore, she clung even more tightly to her son, hiked up her skirts, took to her heels and ran. By the time she came out of her blind panic, it was to the realisation that rather than heading towards her parents' home, as she had intended, she was instead now going back the way she had come earlier. By now within sight of her own home, and already breathless and panting with the exertion and fear, Vera relaxed her hold on her son.

It was at that moment that someone else fleeing from the gun-crazed, rifle-brandishing man, rounded the corner and crashed full tilt into her back before rushing blindly on. The sudden movement pitched her forwards, she stumbled against a low steel garden gate and wee Jamie flew out of her arms and landed with a sickening thud on a stone doorstep. As she looked in horror and listened to her son's screaming, an elderly man just then coming out of his home and descending the stairs, came to her rescue. Tenderly he lifted Jamie up, immediately offered an arm to Vera and having ascertained where she was heading declared that he would see them safely home. As they approached the house, it was to see a knot of people gathered on the pathway.

"Looks like you've got some company, Missus. And a right angry-looking bunch they are. What in the world dae ye suppose all that's about?"

Vera shook her head. "It seems there's trouble at the Sillarmore Bank. But my husband is already down at his Bank, so they're wasting their time in hanging about here, hoping to meet with him."

The man stared at her. "Listen, hen, to my cost I've heard all I want about the Sillarmore bloody Bank this day. If your husband is anything at all to do with that damned Bank, then from here on in, you're on your own. If Ah'd have known ye had any connections with that cheatin, connivin bunch of thieves, I'd have left your son lying on yon doorstep and not have lifted a finger tae help you."

He thrust Jamie back into her arms. But as he turned to leave, he hesitated then speaking behind a cupped hand, he muttered: "Uch, tae hell, ye've been upset enough lassie, so listen, if ye've any sense and if there's a back entrance tae yer hoose, ye'd best make tracks for that. There's some gey angry-looking folk in that mob and they're bayin for somebody's blood."

TEN

The rest of that day seemed endless. Once safely back inside her home, Vera put her son to bed and kept checking on him every half-hour or so. She felt reassured that rather than crying with pain, as might have been expected after such a fall, he was instead sleeping peacefully. Each time she mounted the stairs to his room, she thought, Now this really is when I could be doing with good old Busy Bennet. I wonder how the poor old dear is today. Ah well, no news is good news I reckon.

It was well into the evening before Bob arrived home. As he collapsed into his favourite armchair, he looked up at Vera.

"Thank God I advised you not to venture outdoors today."

Vera could feel herself tense and wondered as to how much or how little she could or indeed should reveal of the day's events. In the end, she decided to play for time and assuming a puzzled look, said: "How do you mean, Bob?"

He passed a weary hand across his brow. "On my way home, I dropped into Belmont Terrace to see how your folks were coping."

Vera smiled. "That was good of you, Bob, I am sure they appreciated that."

The Rich Tapestry of a Tangled Life

Her husband nodded. "True enough but honestly I think what they liked best was having a captive audience to reveal their news of the latest drama even closer to home. Seems like one of their neighbours, a well-respected City gent and a Church Elder, no less, went berserk ... and having somehow got hold of a gun, went screaming out of his house. A danger to himself, the bankers and, of course, anyone else unlucky enough to cross his path."

Vera gasped in horror, aware that now was when she should reveal her own part in the drama. The moment passed and she heard herself say: "What a nightmare. So what did my folks do ?"

Bob took a gulp of neat whisky. "Need you ask? Having caught sight of the armed madman, they did what any sensible person would do ... they barricaded themselves indoors until the danger was past. Of course, I was able to reassure them that acting on my orders, you and wee Jamie were safely at home all day."

There it was again, another, perhaps a final chance, to come right out with it; to tell the truth and shame the devil.

Yet again the moment passed, and Vera said: " How right you were dear, when you forecast ugly scenes. Who would have thought it, a Church Elder running amok with a gun and here in the West End of all places. Beggars belief, doesn't it?"

Bob nodded. "Quite so, my dear. And there are still more evil times ahead. Do you know, all day long there were angry crowds pounding on the door of the Bank."

Vera frowned. "Surely not, dear, what on earth do these people hope to achieve?"

Bob drummed his fingers on the arm of his chair. "Let us not forget, Vera, those investors have lost every penny they had in the world. They want to see someone suffer for their plight. The irony is ... we bank officials and our families, as we already know to our cost, are equally bereft in this crisis."

After a light supper of oatcakes and cheese, for which neither Vera nor Bob had much appetite, on their way upstairs, her husband remarked: "Wee Jamie seems unusually quiet this evening. All right, is he? Like us, I expect he's missing the ministrations of Busy Bennet, Not to mention feeling the effects, the misery, of having been cooped up indoors for the entire day."

ELEVEN

For the rest of that day and night, Vera worried herself sick that her carelessness in letting wee Jamie fall from her arms might as yet in some unseen way have caused him some irremediable damage. Of course if she were being honest with herself, she knew that had the situation been different, then without a doubt she would have enjoined Bob to call out Doctor Nairn to check over the baby and thus put her fears to rest. Feeling tense, not just with the frustration, but with guilt, Vera found herself taking it out on her husband and snapping at him every time he opened his mouth to bewail his many problems at the Bank.

Now in the early light of a new day and seated at the dining-table he looked morosely at the plate which Vera had just placed before him. "Call this a breakfast do you? Heavens above, woman, it's an exact repetition of what we had for so-called dinner last night. Can't you at least drum up a bowl of porridge? Or even boil an egg?"

"You seem to forget you married me not for my culinary skills, but rather more for my social graces and let us not forget as a baby-producing manufactory."

"You're not much good at the latter either, are you?"

Vera gasped in horror and it was a moment before she could bring herself to reply. Then unlike the quiet controlled tone her husband had used, Vera could hear herself yelling like a fishwife. "Listen, Bob, you may be facing a few difficulties at the Bank, but that is no reason to take your frustration out on me. I will not be spoken to in such a manner."

He half-rose from the table to confront her, his face contorted with anger. "Milady, you are my wife and I'll speak to you any damn way I like. And while we're at it, I order you to have a decent meal ready for my return this evening, for I'll have to eat something before I die of malnutrition." With that he stormed out of the house.

As the door banged shut behind him, Vera sat staring unseeingly at the dining-table.

"A decent meal? Damned if I can cook anything, decent or otherwise..."

The sound of Jamie's screams broke into her reverie, alerting her to her duties as a mother.

TWELVE

The balance of the week passed in a haze for Vera. For the first time in her life she found herself in full charge of the running of the household, and all that involved.

As if that weren't enough, she thought, there's also a weeping child longing for his beloved Bentie; distressed parents, now visibly aged and leaning more and more on me; and to cap it all, an increasingly depressed, irritable and hard-to-please husband. Honestly, there's just no pleasing him these days. To hear him talk, anybody would think that the Bank's collapse was all my doing.

As she further reflected on what a foul mood he had yet again been in that morning, and the manner in which he had stormed out of the house, after their latest heated argument, Vera decided that the old adage, a hungry man is an angry man, was probably true, and that she should make some effort with that night's dinner menu.

I know. I'll do a spot of marketing on my way to the Royal to visit Bennet. Kill two birds with one stone.

Once arrived at the Infirmary and seated by the side of Bennet's bed, Vera felt herself compelled to keep up a conversation of some kind to fill the uncomfortable silences between them; silence broken only by the sound of Bennet's laboured breathing and the harsh ticking of the huge wall-mounted clock on the opposite side of the long ward.

In fact, thought Vera, each time she cast another glance at the clock, were it not for its ticking, I'd swear the accursed thing was stuck fast . Honestly, I've never known an hour take such an age to pass. What in God's name can I talk about until the merciful release of that brass bell they clang to announce the end of the official visiting hour?

Like a light dawning in her brain, Vera had an idea.

That's it. I'll talk to her about the art of cooking. That might penetrate the fog in her brain, It might even in some sort of way help speed her recovery. And who knows I might even learn something of use to help me out of my present dilemma in trying to feed Bob.

Vera launched into her monologue. As she rambled on, wondering which if any of her words were getting through to the patient, suddenly Bennet's hands grasped the edge of the red hospital blanket and like a woman possessed she kept intoning the one word over and over: "Haggis, haggis, haggis."

After what seemed an eternity, at last came the clarion call to announce the end of visiting.

The Rich Tapestry of a Tangled Life

"Thank God for that," Vera muttered as she made her way out to the corridor, there to divest herself of the mop-like overshoes, the silence inducers without which no visitor was ever allowed to set foot inside the hallowed wards of healing.

Once arrived back in the West End, Vera collected her son from her parents, gave a brief account of her visit to the Infirmary and was on the point of asking her mother's advice as to the finer points of haggis preparation and cooking when she bit back the words.

Come to think of it, Mother knows even less about cooking than I do and that's saying something. Anyway, surely it can't be all that difficult?

THIRTEEN

By the time Vera had settled her son for the night, prepared the evening meal and set the dining table with extra care, she was already congratulating herself on how really splendidly she was coping and taking in her stride this new lifestyle. It was hours later before Bob finally arrived. One look at his white, anxious face and Vera had no need to ask how his day at the Bank had gone. Even worse, he seemed to have taken a vow of silence, the uncomfortable atmosphere between them was entirely reminiscent of what she had experienced all that miserable afternoon at the Royal.

Hmph, this is even worse, no matron on hand to enforce a strict timetable and put an end to the misery. Never mind, a whisky pre-prandial and then I'm sure the meal will cheer him up, help him relax and lighten this dark cloud of gloom.

Once seated at the table, Bob cast a look of surprise at Vera when she placed a generously-filled plate in front of him .Then without so much as a thank you or even a comment he lifted his knife and fork and at once set to.

Vera watched with interest as he pushed a loaded forkful of food into his mouth.

She gave a sigh of relief as she thought, Nothing to it after all. Who says I couldn't cook?

The Rich Tapestry of a Tangled Life

Bob clattered his cutlery down onto the plate; the sudden movement causing some of the contents of the plate to fly off and land, watery gravy and all, on the pristine white damask tablecloth.

On the point of nagging him, Vera wasn't quick enough.

Bob glared. "I can't eat this muck. At least with the bannocks and cheese the food was recognisable. But this! This disgusting concoction. I don't believe that I even want to know what it's composed of or what in God's name it's meant to be."

Vera could feel tears of anger, frustration and bitter resentment gush into her eyes.

"But, Bob, I tried, I really did. I tried so hard. You'll just have to be patient. Look on this as my apprentice days and just ..."

Her words faded away as he got up with such a sudden movement that his chair overbalanced and crashed to the floor behind him. To add to the uproar, like an avenging Dominie with a recalcitrant pupil he pointed a trembling forefinger at her and bawled: "So you tried did you? That's what you'd have me believe? Well my fine lady, Verity, it's just a f***ing shame you hadn't tried a bloody sight harder."

Vera had never before heard her upright and socially correct husband use such foul language ... and to her. The shock of hearing him address her in this manner stopped her tears, almost as if an unseen hand had turned off the tap.

At the same time, the upset of the entire scene and crude language in some strange way seemed to empower her to stand up for herself.

She looked him fully in the face and said: "While we're on the subject of trying hard, it's just a damned shame that your own paltry efforts at the Bank have failed so miserably. Were it not for that, we would none of us be in this situation ... my parents would not be almost berserk with worry and nor would poor old Bennet be at death's door."

She was on the point of including the horror of Jamie's accident in the street, when reason prevailed and she managed to bite back the words in time.

FOURTEEN

It was a few days later and if anything, the atmosphere between Vera and her husband was even more fraught and all this despite her hard-won, new-found skill at the boiling of eggs: Eggs which could actually be eaten with a spoon rather than drunk from the cup as a white and golden liquid.

The hour of the evening meal had come and gone and still there was no sign of Bob. Just when Vera, having worried and tormented herself with constantly mentally regurgitating all the current frustrations of her life, was on the point of happing up Jamie and going round to her parents, she heard a sound at the door.

"At last," she breathed and her relief in some measure cancelling out the vestiges of their almost ritual breakfast shouting match row, she hurried out into the hallway in readiness to greet him as he would come through the front door. But to her surprise, in the entry, or lobby as Bennet had always colloquially called it, not a sign of her husband was to be seen.

Hmph. I'm getting over-anxious, must have imagined I heard his key in the lock. Ah well, surely he won't be much longer.

She was almost back at the door of the drawing room, when yet again she heard a sound, but this time it was clearly coming from the outer doorway and the little vestibule beyond.

I suppose now he forgot to take his house-keys. Hardly surprising given the foul temper he was in this morning and his hurried departure.

With that thought in mind, she deliberately dawdled her way back to the door, grimly smiling

Serve him right, if I leave him standing out there in the cold for as long as it pleases me before I condescend to admit my so-called lord and master.

Just then the strident doorbell rang out, not once but twice.

Oho, so his lordship does not like to be kept waiting on my convenience. Well, serve him right if I choose to leave him standing out there 'til morning.

However, reason prevailed and albeit with a very bad grace, she finally went to open the door. As the heavy door with its ornamental glass central panel, swung back it was to reveal not Bob, but rather two uniformed figures awaiting her.

"Mistress Drummond?" inquired the more senior-looking of the two men. "May we come in?"

As if holding on to a lifeline, Vera kept a firm grip of the door handle as she tried to make sense of what was happening.

The Rich Tapestry of a Tangled Life

When no sound escaped her lips, the man spoke again: "We are here on official business, so please, may we come in?"

Vera shook her head as light finally dawned. "I'm sorry gentlemen but it rather shook me finding two uniformed policemen on my doorstep. But if as you say, you are on official business ... to do with the Bank, I would imagine ... then sorry but you've had a wasted journey, my husband is still down at the Sillarmore. Perhaps you would like to make an appointment for tomorrow to meet with him at the Bank? Do that and I'll inform my husband the moment he returns."

The two men exchanged meaningful glances. "I'm sorry, but it isn't as simple as that. We have some very bad news to impart."

At once into Vera's mind came vivid mental pictures of the sullen, angry crowds she had seen recently hanging around the Bank's headquarters and, of course, that unforgettable day outside her very own home.

Jumping to conclusions, she said: "Oh, please don't tell me ... that angry mob, they've injured my husband, that's it, isn't it?"

The younger of the two men took a step forward. "Perhaps it would be best if we were to speak indoors, don't you think? Is there another family member on hand?"

Vera shook her head and stood back to admit them.

Inside, the more senior-looking constable suggested that Vera should sit and when she had done so he cleared his throat and said: "Mistress Drummond, there's no easy way to say this. I'm afraid your husband is dead. His body was found in the River Kelvin, just below La Crosse Terrace. Whether he drowned by accident, foul play, or design in a bid to end his own life, as yet we haven't any information."

The younger policeman caught her as she slumped in a faint.

We parted on bad terms. No chance now to apologise. Oh, dear God. What happens now? It was all my fault, I pushed him to the brink. Dear God, help me.

PART TWO

ONE

December 1878

Once into the early days of the month of December, Vera could only gaze in fascinated wonder at the calendar on the wall as she reflected on how drastically her life had changed within the space of only a few short weeks.

"Just as well we never know what lies ahead of us in this life, my girl."

Unaware that she had voiced her thoughts aloud, Vera started in surprise when she heard her father say: "What was that, dear? I didn't quite catch what you said."

Vera turned around in her chair. "Oh, sorry, Father, I didn't mean to disturb. You were dozing over the Glasgow Herald last time I looked."

Her father gave a mirthless laugh. "Dozing indeed. Well, now that you and Jamie have moved in with us I have to take every chance I get of a catnap. Between wee Jamie screaming the place down at night and you and your mother constantly at loggerheads, not to mention you creeping about acting the tragic widow, it's more than a man of my age can stand or should be expected to deal with."

Vera rose to her feet. "Father, that's a terrible thing to say. And to imply that I am faking my sorrow for the loss of my husband, well, words fail me."

Her father rustled his newspaper in a show of impatience. "If words fail you, that's something new, so best keep that particular aspect of your grief for your next encounter with your mother. That way, with any luck, we might all get a bit of peace."

Vera gazed at him in dismay with the yet again stark realisation that the failure of the Bank had indeed affected them all; her father was a changed man. Worst of all in that moment she knew that never again would she be Daddy's wee girl.

On the point of flouncing out of the room, she then thought the better of it. After all if she escaped to the kitchen there would be a pile of dirty dishes awaiting her attention and if she should venture into the drawing room, there she'd be sure to find her mother and baby Jamie.

Vera gave a long heartfelt sigh and in trying to make amends with her father she said: "Anything of special interest in the Herald today, Father?"

He looked up. "Now that you mention it, there was an item that caught my attention. Seems the Lord Provost has proposed some tomfool idea, something about a Municipal treat to cheer up the victims of the Bank crash."

Vera cocked her head on one side. "It's true enough, people are decidedly down in the dumps these days; they could do with a spot of cheering-up. But why on earth would Sir William Collins even think of such an event at this time?"

Her father folded the paper back to the requisite page, then handed it to her with the words: "Here, read it for yourself, Vera. I've seen all I want of it, a waste of public money, if you ask me. Anyway, if this so-called Municipal treat actually comes off, there's only one reason for it, take my word."

"And that is, Father?"

"Stands to reason, with well over eight thousand victims, the authorities are terrified that as it nears Christmas there will be rioting, yes, nothing short of rioting and mob rule in the City streets."

Vera read through the article, then read it again to check the details. "Says here that the cost of the entertainment will be coming from the Lord Provost's private purse. And that he has already detailed a Mister Wattie Freer to organise the entire event which will be held over no less than five of the City's Halls."

Her father snorted in disgust.

"If Sir William Collins can afford to provide a high tea, a substantial high tea no less, free entertainment and a gift going out the door for eight thousand Bank crash victims, then there are two things for sure ..." Vera waited for her father to go on. "Firstly, it's well seen his money didn't come crashing down in the debacle of your husband's Bank and ..."

"And?" Vera prompted, at a loss as to what might be coming. "Secondly, we'll be having no truck with any such charitable hand-outs. The Kilgour family just would not lower themselves thus to appear in public like pathetic downtrodden victims."

Vera stared long and hard at her father. Finally she cleared her throat and in a voice which brooked no argument, she said: "Describe it any way you like, Father, but it seems to have escaped your notice ... we are victims. I have lost my furs, my jewels, my house, my servants, my peace-of-mind, and of course, my husband. If all of that doesn't make me a Bank Crash victim then God alone knows what would. So, as a bona-fide victim, should I wish to accept the invitation to a free Municipal treat, then I for one, damned well will do precisely that."

Her father rose from his chair, the sudden movement somewhat upsetting his balance. Even so, beetle-browed, he thundered: "Verity Kilgour. I forbid, yes, forbid you to do any such thing. You will not bring this family's name into such disgrace. Do you hear me?"

Vera stood up to him. "You're forgetting something, Father, I am now Mistress Verity

Drummond, widow-woman and as of now, I will do exactly as I damn well please. And now goodnight to you, Father."

TWO

On arriving at the City's grandly-named
Wellington Palace, Vera looked around her with
interest. Far from being an ill-assorted mob of
pathetic, poorly dressed, downtrodden victims, in
the main, the guests outwardly at least, appeared
to have somehow held on to one last decent
outfit. Somehow in donning such fine clothes, it
gave them an added confidence; a proud
statement to the world of their human fortitude in
the face of financial ruin. As she took in every
detail of the clothes, and manners of her table
companions Vera was surprised to find that in
such company she felt humbled.

My father was wrong, she thought. I would
not have missed this for anything. Obviously, your
average Glaswegian is made of sterner stuff; the
Glesga sense of humour even in such adversity is
alive and well, and these hardy Clydesiders will rise
above this calamity.

Vera greatly enjoyed the promised substantial
high tea, the free entertainment, and the cheerful
camaraderie of her table companions. As she
collected her commemorative tin of caraway-seed
cake on leaving the event she wondered, would
her father unbend sufficiently to share in eating
the charity gift cake? Even more importantly,

would he consent to letting her try out the sensational idea she'd just had while conversing with fellow bank crash victims at the soiree

I just know that such an idea would not only be an innovation in the annals of any local newspaper, it would arouse interest, hopefully generate advertising revenue and at the same time lift my father's printing business out of the doldrums of this recession. All I have to do now is persuade him.

Throughout the next few days, Vera's father kept referring to the plan Vera had dreamed up and with each question he posed, it was clear that he was gradually coming round to the idea. And this morning was no exception when after a lengthy pause in which he had yet again been mulling it over, he finally said: "Now then, lass, you really do think such a strategy would work?"

Vera pulled her chair nearer to the table. "Father, we have nothing to lose. Apart from anything else and now that mother has more or less taken sole charge of Jamie, I need something to keep me occupied."

He opened his mouth to speak but Vera rushed on: "And listen, Father, if it also gets you out of the house, rather than sitting about here bemoaning your sorrows and instead back to being in charge of things at the print-shop, what could be better?"

No sooner had she finished speaking than with a strange speculative look at her face, he said: "Aye, you've grown up a lot these past couple of months, haven't you, Vera, my lass?"

She nodded. "Needs must when the devil drives, isn't that the saying, Father?" He laughed. "Something like that. Mind you, you've had a lot to cope with, not least of all being put out of the Bank house when poor Bob died."

Vera swallowed hard. "Let's not go into all that right now, Father. It was just a good job that you at least own this house, fully bought and paid for in your own name. Otherwise I'd have been homeless by now."

Not normally given to any great show of emotion, her father's eyes were suddenly awash with tears, then he blew his nose as if like the last trumpet, carefully cleaned his spectacles and assuming a businesslike air, said: "Right. Enough of this idle chitchat, we have work to do. And as you so rightly said, needs must when the devil drives."

THREE

When the notices first appeared in shop windows throughout the city, people were intrigued, amused, scornful and finally motivated to follow up on the strange invitation.

STOP BEING A VICTIM! Rather than being reminded of the Bank Crash every time you look at the now-empty commemorative tin, why not instead turn it into hard cash? Here at the Clarion we promise to pay sixpence for every tin handed in. You'll also get a free copy of the newspaper.

Vera laughed. "To date, our advertisement has brought in quite a few tins and at the same time, just look at the wide publicity the scheme has already generated for the paper."

Her father nodded. "And what keeps the momentum going, people are as intrigued as I am as to what on earth you plan to do with the tins once you have a collection."

"That, of course, is all part and parcel of my master plan. For the moment, having sold my engagement ring and all I had salvaged from my jewellery I can still afford to pay out quite a few sixpences."

"You're a clever girl. Nothing like an air of mystery to whet the appetite. One thing's for sure,Vera, you've got the whole of Glasgow talking, wondering and making wild guesses as to your intentions. It has certainly lifted everyone's spirits in these hard times, given us all a bit of innocent amusement."

Just then Vera's mother came in from her walk.

"Harold. What on earth is going on? Mrs Munro's been telling me and it seems everybody's talking about it, not only are you giving away free, gratis and for nothing, copies of the Clarion, but you are also paying out a fortune in silver sixpences for people's unwanted rubbish. I never heard anything so ridiculous in my life. I told Mistress Munro, in no uncertain manner, that my husband is a newspaper proprietor and not a rag-and-bone-man, thanks all the same."

Vera and her father looked at each other and laughed.

Then answering for her father, Vera said: "Well, Mother, your friend ... or should I say your former friend ... has got a rather garbled version of events. Actually, Father is rather more selective. It's only discarded cake tins he's paying out for, not just any old unspecified rubbish. Isn't that so, Father ?"

The Rich Tapestry of a Tangled Life

One look at her father, by now struggling to contain his laughter showed that he was beyond coherent speech.

"Anyway, Mother, nothing for you to worry your head about it. I can see how much you love having wee Jamie here. And you're both glowing after your walk in the Botanic Gardens. I suspect Mrs Munro was jealous, as yet she has no grandson to parade in the Gardens, and being jealous, she probably said all those things just to upset you."

Another flurry of posters scattered throughout the city, intimating the final date on which the commemorative tins might be purchased by the Clarion, together with the promised free copy of the newspaper, gave a spur of interest to the project.

By the time the due date had come and gone, the front offices of the Clarion resembled nothing so much as an overfilled warehouse ... a warehouse whose only commodity was empty commemorative tins. And since as yet Vera had not discussed her plans for such items, everyone, her father included, was agog with curiosity.

When the Clarion office closed on the Friday as usual at twelve-thirty after the weekly publication of the newspaper, Vera worked hard for the rest of the day and throughout the entire Saturday. At last she was finished. The large front window by then housed a massive display of the tins, the only difference now being that each tin bore a clearly-printed number. When on the Saturday evening, she showed off her handiwork to her father, he scratched his head in obvious puzzlement.

"Oh, aye, lass, it all looks very artistically arranged, I grant you that ... but what in the name of the wee man do all those garish numbers stand for? It fair beats me, and I do consider myself to be a reasonably intelligent man."

Vera laughed. "No need to be so modest, Father. Reasonably intelligent, my Granny. Who was the brains behind getting the Clarion up and running all those years ago?"

Over a welcome cup of tea, Vera explained precisely what she had in mind.

"As of the next issue, there will be no more free copies of the newspaper and the cost will be going up by a halfpenny. The newspaper will carry each week a random selection of numbers, each of which will correspond to a number on a tin. The contents in the tins will vary from week to week ... for instance one week a reader who first claims tin number three will find a golden sovereign awaiting him at the office. Then the next week, number three might house a bag of flour, another time, complimentary tickets to the Variety and so on. I'm sure you get the idea, Father."

"Indeed I do, lass. Well done. If I could add an extra idea ... if we publish the names of the winners, even more people will buy the paper, for folk love to see their names in print."

Vera grinned. "I always said you were the brains in this outfit, Father."

FOUR

Despite her father's misgivings, over the increased cover price of the newspaper, circulation soared to previously undreamt-of heights.

It seemed as if everyone with an eye to business jumped on the bandwagon of free publicity. This meant that scarcely a week passed but what a local butcher, baker, coal merchant or Variety Theatre proprietor would gift a wee something for the tins. As long as such benefactors were given due and prominent mention in the Donors' List, they in turn were well satisfied with such public recognition.

While Vera and her father were mutually congratulating each other on the flyaway success of the Clarion, Vera always made sure to include her mother's contribution, without which, namely her care of wee Jamie, Vera would not otherwise have had the freedom to pursue such an untrammelled business career. This evening as the family sat together in the Grange and the success of the Clarion had yet again been lauded to the skies, her mother suddenly said: "Perhaps now that business matters are once again moving , there's a couple of points I'd like to raise."

At once Mrs Kilgour had their undivided attention.

The Rich Tapestry of a Tangled Life

"First of all, I do think we could well afford again the services of a live-in tweenie."

Her husband nodded his ready acceptance of this modest request and thus encouraged, his wife went on: " Further to that. Bennet is due out of hospital next week and I want to bring her here to live in this house. Not that initially she'll be of much use on the domestic front, I grant you, but at least she could sit with and supervise wee Jamie. He's now very demanding and it would give me a well-earned break, perhaps even a bit of social life. What do you think?"

Mr Kilgour beamed. "Can't say I find a problem with any of that."

Vera pursed her lips: "Just one thing, Mother, when you say Jamie is more demanding ... I mean, he is all right. isn't he?"

Her mother frowned. "What a thing to ask, Vera. He's a normal child. Of course he's all right. He's my grandson, no reason why he should be otherwise than perfectly normal in his development." She paused for a moment, then with a reflective look on her face, she said: "Of course, it does have to be said, in many things he's a wee bit slower than you were as a child at his age. But nothing, absolutely nothing wrong, with him, I do assure you."

FIVE

1879

One morning after breakfast, Vera's father threw down in disgust his copy of the Glasgow Herald. "Vera you're never going to believe what I've just been reading."

Vera laughed. "Well, not unless you deign to tell me what you're on about."

"Point taken lass, point taken. All right, the gist of the matter is this, some young upstart of a fellow, somebody called Thomas Lipton, not long since arrived back from America, if you please, he's only just opened a discount grocery store ... whatever the devil that might be ... but opened it in Finnieston, not exactly the West End, now is it?"

Vera smiled. "Well, good luck to the lad, whoever he may be. Nothing wrong in that surely, now is there?"

Her father snorted. "I'll tell you what's wrong ... seems he has taken to concealing golden sovereigns inside a giant cheese, he then sells slices of it to hopeful people who stand out in the public street tearing their portions of cheese apart in search of hidden treasure, gobbling it down before they dash into his discount shop in search of more illgotten gains. There now, what do you think of that for a bit of cheek?"

Vera frowned. "I still don't see ... oh, wait a minute, you don't mean to say you think he has copied our idea; the treasure tins, only in his case, its treasure wads of cheese?"

Her father nodded and a silence ensued.

Finally Vera laid a comforting hand on his arm. "I wouldn't worry unduly. This Thomas Lipton, whoever he is, just a flash in the pan. Newly arrived from America, you say, and probably thinks he knows it all. Hardworking Clydesiders won't fall for such a ruse for too long, after all there is a limit to the amount of cheese any one person can either afford or for that matter, even stomach in the hope of ever finding a sovereign."

Her father stroked his beard in contemplation. "Aye, you're right, Vera, such a fly-by-night is no competition for the Clarion ... after all, let's face it, our Treasure Tins were here first and by now they are a well-established facet of Glasgow life. Nothing can change that."

1880

It was now two years since the horrendous shock of the Sillarmore Bank crash. In that time, of the eight thousand or so victims, some had arisen from the ashes; others were still scrabbling to gain a foothold on the ladder of financial stability; and still other victims had despairingly given up the unequal struggle as totally beyond their understanding or endurance. As these thoughts went through Vera's mind, she reflected on how blessed she and her family were. Now that they were all living under the same roof in Belmont Crescent with the household running smoothly enough, with Jamie in the care of his Gran and his beloved Bentie, peace reigned, thus enabling Vera and her father to go off, free and untrammelled to work each day at the Clarion .

One morning in going through the day's post, Vera was surprised on opening a rather expensive-looking envelope to find that it contained a very special invitation. Having read the words for a second time, she called across the office to her father. "Father, you'll never believe what we've be invited to attend ... the launching of the Livadia."

At once her father crossed the floor to stand beside her as he read the ornate, gold-edged card for himself. Having perused it carefully, he laughed. "An invitation from Admiral Popoff himself, no less. I expect like everyone else, they're looking for additional free publicity."

Vera smiled. "No doubt, but if we can't exactly put the Livadia into one of our treasure tins, at least, we can give the event something of a mention in the paper."

Her father nodded. "Well, since half the City of Glasgow is talking and in a flurry of excitement about the luxury yacht built at Fairfields for the Czar of all the Russias, yes, why don't we run an article about this floating palace."

"Mind you, when I first heard the name of the Admiral in charge of the project, as we Glaswegians would put it ... I thought somebody was takin a len of me."

"You're right, my dear, the worthy gentleman does go by the name of Admiral Popoff. So make sure you get the spelling right when you accept his kind invitation."

Vera's eyes opened wide in surprise. "You really mean we're going? After all in this line of business, we must get dozens of invitations to all sorts of events ... everything from Bonnie Baby Contests, to Gala Openings of the latest shopping arcade."

"True enough, lass, but this is one invitation I wouldn't miss for the world. Anyway, you'll enjoy it and in years to come, it'll be something to tell your grandchildren."

"Father, do you think it's true; has the Livadia really got a rose garden, sparkling illuminated fountains, a ballroom, and wine racks enough to house ten thousand bottles of wine?"

Her father patted her hand. "One way to find out. As guests of the Admiral, we'll visit the 'summerhouse on a raft' and see for ourselves."

On the day of the launching, it seemed as if the entire population of Glasgow was in holiday mood and had congregated in Govan for Fairfield Yard's send off to the world's most expensive, most luxurious private yacht. On all sides small boys in sailor suits, their caps emblazoned with the word Livadia were running around in a high state of excitement; old ladies were waving flags; people who could hardly walk due to the ravages of age, the demon drink or physical infirmity, were marching along in ragged lines between pipe bands.

Ensconced in the select company of the Platform Party, Vera's father turned to her and said: "I'm glad this is one invitation we accepted, lass. Surely a day to remember."

"Indeed Father and well worth the time and money I expended on this new outfit. Although, looking and listening to such exuberance all around us, it does give me pause to wonder ..." Her father waited for her to go on.

"It's just ... well ... somehow, when I see all this hilarity and reflect on the obscene sums of money needed to build this rich man's toy, I can't help thinking about the on-going poverty and misery of the Sillarmore's collapse. For me, it's too big a contrast to make any sense. I just cannot comprehend it."

Her father shook his head.

"You worry too much, Vera, it's always been the case that this world is unevenly divided, but what today proves to me is that Glasgow is alive and well. Glaswegians can and do rise above any

and all adversity and they do not for a moment
begrudge the Czar of all the Russias, his good
fortune. So why don't you relax and enjoy the
event and make the very best of today?" Thus
empowered by her normally rather sedate father
to forget the misery of the Sillamore debacle, to
cast worry and fret aside, and enjoy what currently
was on offer, Vera did exactly that.

SIX

Now here she was many months later still enjoying the fruits of that carefree day.

As she and Gavin Reid sat over the dessert course of an excellent meal in the newly-refurbished Grand Hotel at Charing Cross, her escort smiled and said: "You know, Vera, the strange thing is, I very nearly did not attend that Platform Party invitation. To me, the very idea of Scottish workmen having to construct that rich man's toy, with then having to go home each night to mouse-infested, rat-ridden hovels of a single-end, in Govan or Partick was obscene."

Vera studied the face of the handsome widower sitting across the table from her. "Then why did you accept the invitation if the concept was all so abhorrent to you?"

He puffed out his cheeks. "Like so many things in life, in the last analysis, it all came down to money, not forgetting the contacts one can make at such a gathering. I figured if those skilled workmen could forget their own pitiful living conditions and yet still give of their best, then why couldn't I?"

Vera grinned. "So you're now telling me that you too live in squalid conditions? Not exactly how I would be inclined to describe a handsome town house in Great Western Road. But I suppose it's all relative, isn't it?"

He stretched forward over the table and placing a pinky-ringed hand over hers, said: "One of the things I like about you, Verity, you are totally honest; you say what you think and, God help me, you continually miss the point I'm trying to propound."

Vera looked down at where his hand still rested on her own.

After a reflective pause, she said: "Actually, that's three points you've detailed. But come to think of it, I was unaware that you liked anything about me."

He laughed. "Now who's fishing for compliments, my dear? But joking aside, when I saw you at the launch, wearing that ridiculous hat, complete with peacock feathers, bobbles and beads and every other artifice known to man, I at once decided that rather then being a sedate Scottish matron, you were one of Admiral Popoff's ladies. So it's a wonder I even summoned up the nerve to speak to you."

At these words, Vera gave such a hearty, unbridled laugh that the couple at a nearby table, turned their heads and gave her a rather sour look. If anything this added to Vera's amusement, but even so, she felt compelled to lower her voice somewhat. "So, in other words, you took your time before deciding it was safe to approach me .And in which particular category of womanhood did you finally place me: sedate Scottish matron or as you so delicately put it, one of Admiral Popoff's ladies?"

Gavin grinned almost boyishly as if caught out in some misdemeanour. "Actually, my dear, it would be a brave man who would attempt to categorise you, Verity Drummond. You are in a class of your own: newspaper proprietor, widowed mother, carer of aged parents, and family retainer, king-pin of the Kilgour family, clan more like. Need I say more?"

"Just one thing you missed out, you forgot to mention predatory widow."

"It's just a pity that such a label does not apply to you, otherwise by now you would have accepted my monthly proposal of marriage. Anyway, no predatory widow on the hunt for a man would have been seen dead in that ridiculous hat you wore at Livadia's launching."

Vera leant further forward in her seat. "Ridiculous hat or not, it worked its magic with you, did it not?"

"Is that by way of telling me that you accept my hand in marriage?"

Vera shook her head. "Not so fast. Gavin. Given my many responsibilities, I just cannot abandon them as and when I please. But one thing I promise you, when I do say 'Yes', you will be left in no doubt as to my intention."

"Fair enough but I'll be equally honest with you. I'm much older than you. I want a wife and companion now and although to date I have not mentioned it, but God willing, I would like to have sons to inherit my business, my properties and all the materially good things I've accumulated from my own hard work over the years. Like it or not, but time marches on and so time is of the essence."

Vera frowned as she thought, Speak now or forever hold your peace.

Then deciding that honesty was the best policy, she said: "Gavin let me say that if you are looking for a wife to be mother to your hypothetical sons, then that is one role for which I am most definitely not suited. Rather an indelicate subject, but according to the medical fraternity, I am incapable of bearing even one more child."

Instead of the crestfallen look she had anticipated, Gavin beamed his delight at hearing such news. "Vera, my dear, at my age and enjoying the quiet life as I do, I really do not want to be encumbered with teething babies, sleepless nights and all the paraphernalia that goes with them. I've seen enough of all that with my sister's brood and ..."

Vera interrupted him. "Then why on earth mention that you wanted sons? I just do not understand."

Again he reached for her hand which at the height of their discussion, she had hastily withdrawn. "The point is, I was actually thinking of you, my dear, I didn't want you to feel that you would be missing out on having a new family if you were to marry a man of my age. You and I get on very well together, companionship, that's what is so important. And, of course, should you consent to marry me, then I would legally adopt your son. Jamie's a fine laddie and he would be all the son and heir I would ever want."

SEVEN

1881

The newspaper had been put to bed for another week and Vera and her parents were relaxing over a cup of tea in the drawing room. Deciding that this was as good a time as any to break the news of her prospective engagement, Vera cleared her throat then said: "Gavin Reid again proposed to me last night. I've said I'll give him my answer next week."

Her mother stared wide-eyed. "Hmph, I'll never understand you, Verity, why the delay? It takes only the merest second to say 'No'."

Vera replaced her cup on its saucer. "Oh Mother, really You're not about to start all that again Anyway, despite your views on the matter, Gavin must have some social standing in polite circles. How else was he an invited member of the official launch party? Don't forget that's where I first met him. For your information, Gavin Reid is a perfectly decent, well-heeled respectable man of business."

Her mother bridled. "Man of business indeed. I never heard such nonsense. He's in trade. All right he owns a chain of fish shops but even so, I ask you .... you the widow of a bank manager. Could you really lower yourself socially to become the wife of a fishmonger? For all I know, he even started out by wheeling a fish barrow through the streets of Glasgow." Vera snapped. "Actually, that was his mother who started the business in that way."

Mrs. Kilgour gave a gasp of horror. "This gets worse by the minute ... do you mean to tell me his own mother was a cloth-capped, wheelbarrow-pushing fishwife, with the requisite bugle to announce her wares, part and parcel of the Glasgow street-scene. Just the tiniest degree higher socially than any equally raucous ragwife."

Before Vera could reply, her father entered the debate. "Much as I hate to admit it, Vera, but your mother is right. It would scarcely be fitting for someone in your social position to have a fishwife, retired or not, as a mother-in-law."

"Social position be damned." Scarcely had Vera spoken than Mrs. Kilgour said: "Verity, that is no way to speak to your father. Anyway, talking of fish, if you ask me, there's something decidedly fishy about a man who prospered after the bank's collapse, when the rest of Glasgow was penniless and on its knees."

Mr, Kilgour nodded. "I'm inclined to agree with your mother, Verity. Look how the bank's collapse affected us."

Vera got to her feet. "Perhaps Gavin did learn a trick or two from his fishwife mother .... they did not ever entrust their hard-earned money to banks, far less invest in stocks and shares. as you yourself did, Father. No, an old shortbread tin under the bed for them .... that's how they survived and, of course, let us not forget ... what still earns him a daily crust ... as part of a healthy diet , most folk do on occasion eat fish."

As she started to walk towards the door, Vera stopped when she heard her mother say: "Call me a snob if you like, Verity but I could not hold my head up socially nor at the Church were you to become the wife of a fishmonger. Why not marry a coalminer and be done with it? At least miners and their families traditionally have their own separate stairways to Church galleries. So no unfortunate mixing involved with our social inferiors there."

Vera turned to face her mother. "Thank you, Mother, for your inestimable help in my reaching a firm decision. Actually, I'd had it in mind to refuse Gavin's proposal of marriage, and that's what I was about to tell you, but now? Yes, I do see things more clearly and in a totally different light. As you pointed out, as a rich man, Gavin will be an excellent provider and foster stepfather for my son. Who knows, in time Jamie might even get to like fish and one thing is sure, neither he nor I will ever go hungry."

PART THREE

ONE

April 1882

The day of Vera and Gavin's wedding was in direct contrast to that of her first marriage, when even the weather had seemed to bless the event. Today with the West of Scotland rain doing its best to drown the newly-wed happy couple never had the environs of Glasgow looked more bleak and less inviting.

The bride and groom with their sparse group of attendants, made their way into the Grand Hotel for a celebratory meal. None of the usual trappings of a society wedding meal were present. Today there was a small tier-less cake with not a favour in sight, and one table sufficed to seat the bride and groom and their invited number of guests.

Seated next to her new husband, as she looked round the assembled guests, Vera thought, Just as well my mother pleaded a bilious attack as her excuse to miss the wedding, she could never have competed with the elegance of Gavin's Paris-gowned mother.

The Rich Tapestry of a Tangled Life

Almost as if by thought transference, Gavin's mother ... 'Just call me Lizzie' ... looked across at Vera and smiled.

In that instant, Vera thought that smile, her regal demeanour, and even the outrageously expensive outfit, every feathery flounce and flurry of which screamed money, says it all. Good old Lizzie, she's so, happy that her ageing son has at last got himself another wife ... what was it she said? Oh yes, Gavin has already devoted too much of his life to work, to building up his shops all over Glasgow, and too many years in taking care of his old Mammy.

About to pursue this line of thinking even further, Vera came back to the here and now of reality when her father started on his speech of welcome to the guests, to Mrs Reid senior and to his new son-in-law.

Later that evening as the guests were going their separate ways and the newly-weds were setting off on a short honeymoon to be spent at the seaside town of Largs, her father took Vera aside to say in a voice choked with emotion "You deserve all the happiness in the world, lass. Don't worry about Jamie, in your absence your mother and Bennet, will take good care of him. And although you can't see it now, in time, your mother will come around to accepting your new husband."

Jenny Telfer Chaplin

April 1884

Gavin looked fondly at Vera across the breakfast table. "It hardly seems possible, does it, dear? In another couple of days it will be our second wedding anniversary."

"Even more remarkable, not only does my nother now actually look the road you're on, but yet again she's determined to make a big fuss of our anniversary. She still feels guilty about her boycott of our wedding – bilious headache, indeed. You know, I wouldn't be surprised if nowadays she even boasts to her friends: 'My son-in-law, he owns a chain of shops, you know, just like that up-n-coming Mr Thomas Lipton.'"

Gavin laughed. "Don't be too hard on your mother, Vera. She was brought up to be a snob. Anyway, I think what finally brought her round to look more kindly on me was when we mutually agreed that although I'm legally adopting Jamie, he could go on living with them at Belmont Crescent – handier after all, now that he's at the Academy –and that he could always visit with us for high days and holidays."

"True enough, she and Bennet, they'd have been lost without Jamie, And this arrangement, it gives me time to help Father occasionally with the newspaper and of course to be here at home for your Mum. And not forgetting also to be at your right hand for our rather hectic social life."

The Rich Tapestry of a Tangled Life

Gavin lifted the pile of envelopes from the morning's post. "Talking of which, this looks like another lot of invitations, I'll let you attend to that later this morning, shall I?"

As they rose from the table about to start their day, Vera said: "By the way, Lizzie mentioned to me that she's been invited yet again to meet up with my mother's sewing ladies for an afternoon bun fight. What do you suppose that's all about?"

Gavin grinned. "You mean apart from their usual vast consumption of cakes and buns? Seriously, your mother just may have taken to heart the sob story I told her ..."

Vera frowned. "Gavin, what have you been up to?"

He put a hand on her arm. "You really want to know? Well, I appealed to your mother's sense of fairness and her obvious and well-entrenched feelings of social superiority ..."

Vera gave a hollow laugh. "As to her sense of fairness, I didn't know she had one."

"Verity, that's unkind Anyway, do you or do you not want to hear my story?"

"I can hardly wait."

Gavin cleared his throat. "Let's sit down. Right, here goes. I know that she has always looked down on my mother. No, don't deny it. So I called on Mrs Kilgour's sense of being kind to the underprivileged like the lady of the manor with her cottagers and ... I simply told her, in the strictest of confidence, of course, that my mother was deeply conscious of her own lack of social graces, had no social chitchat whatsoever, but she was an excellent listener. As such, she would be an asset, an expensively dressed asset, to any gathering of socially correct and upwardly ambitious women. That was it; that was all it took ... the rest as they say is history." Vera grinned. "So far so good. dear husband, but I rather think there's something more, some facet of this saga you're not telling me."

Looking like a naughty child caught out in some misdemeanour he said: "Honestly, Vera, you can read me like a book. Truth is, and I must stress this is for your ears alone, I paid for some elocution lessons for my dear old Mammy and a real bool-in-mooth minor royal, working for a pittance has now trained her to say very politely, with the most perfect diction: 'How very interesting, that's nice' To the boast of every boring social climber she meets ... whereas in the past my Calton-bred Mammy's instinct and habit of a lifetime, with the Glasgow accent well to the fore would have been to tell such bumchattin snobbish timewasters 'to f ... off' and 'Haud yer wheesht and just f ... off'." Whereas now she listens politely, then cut-glass accent to the fore, she smiles sweetly with her expensive new wallies, and says, 'How very interesting, that's nice'. Certainly more acceptable in polite society and worth every halfpenny it cost me for the elocution lessons."

TWO

1885

With Gavin having a fish shop in just about every district in Glasgow and with his innate kindness and charitable work, this meant that scarcely a week passed but what there would be an invitation to some local event or other. In discussing this aspect of their life together, Gavin smiled. "Come to think of it, my dear, that was how I first met you, when I was invited to the Livadia launch party. I'll never forget that ridiculous ..."

"Don't you dare. I never want ever to hear another word about my party hat. To think it cost me an absolute fortune at Madam Aimee's from her exclusive salon in Sauchiehall Street , in the window of which she only ever displayed one item. Anyway, I'm sure I wasn't the only widow woman you met that day?"

"True enough. There was also Mrs Isabella Elder, the widow of the famous Fairfields Shipbuilder, John Elder. And as you know, even though she didn't have a sufficiently eye-catching hat with which to capture me, at least the dear lady still does keep in touch with us from time to time."

The Rich Tapestry of a Tangled Life

It was just a couple of days later that on reading an ornate invitation card, Vera said: "Now there's a coincidence."

Looking up from behind his spread newspaper, Gavin said rather absently: "What? What's that, dear?"

"Just the other day, you happened to mention the name of Mrs Isabella Elder. Well, now here she is writing to invite us to the Gala Opening of Elder Park, which it seems she has gifted to the people of Govan as a fitting memorial to her late husband."

Gavin laid down his paper. "Yes, her husband was only forty-five years of age when he died, a man of wonderful humanitarian beliefs and principles. And his widow has already, over the past sixteen years or so, since his untimely death, given much to the people of Govan and to Glasgow. Anyway, what's this you say about Elder Park?"

"It seems the Elder Park is to be officially opened on Saturday twenty-seventh of June, by none other than the Right honourable the Earl of Roseberry. Wait 'til my mother hears of this. But what do you think of that, dear?"

Gavin laid down his newspaper, grinned boyishly and said: "What I think is that my dear lady wife will look on this occasion as a splendid excuse for a wildly expensive new outfit, and, of course, an afternoon in the company of Madame Aimee in the search of an eye-catching new...."

Before he could finish his sentence, Vera rushed over to him, placed a silencing hand across his mouth and gave him a warm embrace.

SATURDAY 27th June, 1885

As Gavin and Vera, dressed in best bib and tucker drove in their carriage through the streets of Govan, on their way to the opening ceremony, on all sides the streets were dressed overall in flags, bunting and banners bearing such mottoes as:

> Peace and pleasure to our noble Donor.
> All honour to Mrs Elder
> Her name shall live forever.

The local Indian tea bazaar, artistically-draped with evergreens, bore on its window the legend: "With Elder Park and Bazaar Tea, Govan now content should be."
The walls of tenement buildings and many another shop front sported such verse as:

> Every person must agree
> That Govan now content should be
> A handsome park they've got free.

With pipe bands skirling, people cheering, notabilities speechifying and children dancing along, caught up in the excitement, the Gala

The Rich Tapestry of a Tangled Life

Opening of Elder Park was most certainly a day to remember. As they eventually made their way home, Gavin turned to Vera and said: "A fitting tribute indeed to Isabella's late husband. As one speaker pointed out on his rather lengthy address, the Elder Park will serve in promoting the happiness and refinement of the people."

"Yes, I'm sure that's true enough and it certainly promoted my happiness. I love my new outfit. When I tell my mother that none other than the Earl of Roseberry himself, actually spoke to me, complimented me on my modish gown, well, I tell you, my dear mother will dine out on that titbit of socially correct gossip for months to come. I can hear her already ... 'My daughter was just saying to Lord Roseberry ...'"

Gavin laughed, and gave her hand a squeeze. "Vera, not only do you have a vivid imagination but you can have a very sarcastic edge to your tongue when you mention your mother."

"Yes, thank you, I do know, I'm well aware of that aspect of my character, you've told me often enough. But you love me just the same, don't you dear?"

As Gavin led her into their home, he laughed. "That remains to be seen. but before we retire to bed, I'll tell you one thing ... we'll not get a moment's peace alone until you sit with my mother, give another twirl and tell her all about our big day out at the Elder Park."

THREE

1892

The years moved on and with each wedding anniversary, Vera blessed the day she had consented to marry Gavin Reid.

If ever a marriage was made in heaven, she thought, it was surely this one, we are so well suited, we have a wonderful life together and with Lizzie here in the house with us, nobody ever had a better or more kindly mother-in-law."

Vera was still sitting motionless before her dressing table mirror when Gavin came into the bedroom and laying a hand on her shoulder, he said: "Still debating as to which of your many stylish outfits to wear for tonight's anniversary party?"

"Actually, I was wondering how on earth you've managed to live with me all these years, coped with what Bennet used to call my 'miffties' and yet you still come up smiling."

Gavin turned her round to face him. "I'd never heard of dark moods being referred to as 'miffties' before I met you. Anyway, it isn't every bride in the land who'd have welcomed an old fishwife mother-in-law into the marital home. So one way and another, I'd say we suit each other and have adapted to each other's needs very well."

Then as he turned to leave the room, he said: "Now then, lass, high time you were into your party frock. My mother is already all toshed up for the big event and rarin to go. You do know what a stickler for good timekeeping your mother is."

Arrived at Belmont Crescent, it was at once clear that her mother and Bennet had been hard at work to prepare for the party.

Everything was gleaming, the ribbon-garlanded dining table was a work of art and sixteen-year-old Jamie, now in his final year at the Academy, had been pressed into buttling service for the big event. Altogether, it was a real family affair, alive with laughter, good humour and a host of shared memories. Later, the anniversary cake with its ten candles having been well sampled, they all gathered round the piano in the drawing room for a singsong. Then having gone through the repertoire of Scottish and Irish favourites, old and new, there was a pause in which Mrs Kilgour said: "Now, by special request a little party-piece which Lizzie and I have been practising over many an afternoon for this past month or so. Ready when you are Lizzie."

Mrs Kilgour thumped out a rallentando on the keys of the piano, as a dramatic introduction , at which time Lizzie, as to the manner born, executed a rather wobbly curtsey. Then launching into the words of their rehearsed composition, she sang: "How very interesting, how very interesting, how very interesting, that's nice. Your boasts with me they cut no ice, and so I say, How very interesting, that's nice."

From the thunderous applause and shrieks of laughter, which greeted this, it was clear that the long-suppressed so-called secret of Lizzie's elocution lessons was a secret no longer. And somehow this revelation gave the seal of approval to the wonderful feeling of camaraderie which a few short years ago would have been utterly unthinkable in such a company.

As the trio arrived home at Grosvenor Terrace, a tired but happy Lizzie was all set to go upstairs with all possible speed to bed, when Gavin delayed her with the words: "Not so fast. Mammy, You were the star of the show tonight. Vera agrees with me as did all the other guests, so a wee nightcap in the drawing room, will round off the evening for all of us. And you can even have a long lie tomorrow."

Lizzie's eyes sparkled. "Yes, it's been a real hoolie of a day."

As the mourners were leaving from the funeral tea, the general consensus was that while Lizzie's sudden demise was undoubtedly a cruel blow to those that are left, nevertheless it was that very same suddenness that surely came as a blessing to the old lady. As one equally aged friend further expounded the theory, there was much nodding of agreement from white-haired mourners that just to go to sleep after a pleasant day spent with one's family, and never to waken up again ... no pain, no misery, no dying an inch at a time from some dread disease ... who could ask for a greater release from life's journey?

In the aftermath of Lizzie's death there were several surprises for Gavin and Vera. The first of these was a letter which arrived from a respected City firm of solicitors requesting their attendance at the Reading of the Will. Having read the letter, Gavin turned to Vera with a puzzled frown on his face. "I can't understand this. A will? My mother never had any dealings with lawyers, bankers or any such. As you know, her fail-safe bank was a tin under the bed."

"True enough. but as you said, the contents of the tin were sadly depleted lately, given her penchant for expensive clothes. Anyway, no doubt the solicitor will enlighten us. What date are we expected at his office?"

On the appointed day, having listened with growing amazement to the contents of the Will, it was a rather stunned husband and wife who later walked through the City streets.

"Why on earth would my mother have bought an old weaver's cottage, and in Largs of all places? And according to the solicitor, she'd never even seen the place. All sounds a great mystery to me."

"Well, as to the Largs bit ... that I can understand. Remember after our honeymoon there, we raved on about the wonderfully bracing air, the uncluttered seafront, the boats plying to and fro across to Millport. Remember?"

"Yes, my dear, of course, and I also recall my mother's delight in our happiness. So I suppose, one way and another, the idea of that particular seaside town must have stuck in her mind." Vera nodded thoughtfully. "And now I come to think of it, I seem to recall hearing my father in full oratorical spate, in the light of his own stocks and shares fiasco, going on about bricks and mortar being the safest haven for anyone's hard-earned money."

"I am beginning to see daylight."

"At the first opportunity you, or we, should journey to Largs to see your inheritance ... Gateside Cottage."

PART FOUR

ONE

1894

In the two years following Lizzie's death, the wee cottage in Largs became a wonderful weekend and holiday escape for Vera and her husband each time they needed a breather from their busy lives in Glasgow. Although not given to voicing his fears, with each year that passed, Gavin was feeling the weight of his age and starting to daydream about retiring to "our wee seaside cottage". If Vera were being honest, on the odd occasion he did hint about a possible early retirement, she never actually encouraged him in such fanciful plans, knowing full well that she enjoyed to the limit the lifestyle they already had. No sooner had she been mentally congratulating herself on managing to keep things on a even keel than suddenly it seemed not only had her world been turned upside down, but worst of all, had been wrenched from her own hands that very day.

She glared at her son and said: "And we all know who's to blame for that, don't we, Jamie? If you'd gone on to study at the University as I'd intended you should those years ago, none of this present situation would have arisen. You would not now be slouching around as an unemployed, indeed unemployable glorified office junior."

Just then Gavin interrupted. "Now then, dearest, don't be too hard on the laddie. If you must know, play our cards right and this could actually be a blessing in disguise."

Vera turned angrily to face her husband. "Indeed, and just precisely how do you arrive at that conclusion?"

Gavin waved her to a seat with the words: "Suppose we all sit down, keep calm and discuss our future plans in a civilised manner. Let's face it, in the final outcome, Jamie here will inherit all my shops anyway, and since the world of Academe holds no attraction for him ... nor for that matter does any other line of occupation he's tried so far ... why shouldn't he get into the fishmongery business sooner, rather than later? It all makes sound common sense to me."

Vera pursed her lips. "Well, then, by the same token , my own father is not all that much older than you, why shouldn't he retire and hand over the reins of the print shop to the same callow youth?"

"The difference there is that your father still enjoys working. It gets him out of the house and out from under the feet of your mother and Busy Bennet. If I were in your father's shoes, I'd be exactly the same and happy to work all the hours that God sends."

"Oh well, Gavin, have it your own way, throw away everything you've worked for all your life and go and bury yourself in that mouldy old cottage. But I for one will not be joining you."

As Vera finished speaking, Gavin stared hard at her then said: "Vera, I am tired of working and since God has blessed us with the happy marriage we share, it stands to reason, I'd want us to enjoy some of the fruits of hardworking years ... not only of mine, but also of my dear departed mother. Can you possibly ever imagine the harsh reality of what Lizzie's life must have been in the early days, when as a widow, with a young son to bring up, she had to earn a living somehow. And many a bitterly cold winter's morning, she'd give me my porridge, trail me with her around the streets until it was time for school. How else do you think I ever learned about the fishmongery business in the first place?"

As he finished speaking, Vera having mentally imagined the scene was already in tears.

"So, if it means all that much to you to have me by your side in Largs ...?"

Gavin grinned his delight, secure in the knowledge that a crisis in their marriage had been averted. "There it is, Jamie, and from what I gather at the look of horror on your face when there was a suggestion that your future might lie at the print-shop, I'm assuming that it's the fishmongery business for you. But mind you, you'll start at the bottom, same as I did, I'll give you a year to settle into it. Fine, then. I'll get my solicitor to draw up the essential legal documents. Once it's all settled, the business and this house will all be in your name."

On the point of shaking hands on the deal, they both gave a start when Vera, pointing an admonitory finger at her husband, yelled in a voice totally unlike her usual ladylike tones. "Gavin have you taken leave of your senses? My agreeing to spend time with you in Largs is one thing, and giving Jamie a job in the shops is another, but rightly or wrongly I had assumed that we'd still own this beautiful house, and once you were fully retired we could come and go between the seaside and Grosvenor Terrace as and when, if we wanted a change of scenery."

Gavin put out a placatory hand but Vera would have none of it.

"Good heavens, all right, he's my son, but I'd be the first to point out in the two years since he left the Academy ... no qualifications of any kind ... unless you count a certificate for good attendance, has not been able to hold down any job, far less show the slightest inclination to work. And yet, here you are not only happy to hand over, after a brief apprenticeship, the reins of your business, but also handing him the key of this magnificent house, here in the West End. Have you taken leave of your senses?"

The Rich Tapestry of a Tangled Life

Gavin frowned. "That's enough, Vera, the matter is settled."

"But—"

"But me no buts, Vera, there is nothing else to be said."

Vera glared at her husband, then after a speculative look at her son, she took a deep breath. "Actually, there is something else, the one thing you obviously do not know, not one other person in the world is aware of this except myself ..."

She had the fixed attention of them both. "I have never told this to another living soul, nor indeed will I ever again refer to it after today, but I think you have to be told, Gavin, before the pair of you go waltzing off to any solicitor. As a baby, my son was dropped on his head. So who knows, perhaps that accident could well account for his inability to concentrate on work, or even on any meaningful leisure time occupation. Let's face it, he's not correct, now is he? Not the full twenty shillings in the pound. Sorry, Jamie, I had hoped to keep such childhood history from you all your life, but at least now it's out in the open, it could explain a great deal, don't you think?"

Jamie and his stepfather, having heard her out turned to each other and Gavin said: "That is utterly despicable for any mother to say such a thing or to make up such terrible lies about her own son, just for the sake of keeping her hold on a Georgian town house. I never heard the likes.

Sorry, Vera, but I refuse to believe a word of it, and that is the end of the matter, never again will we refer to such a damning indictment on your son. The way you are going on, it seems to me if anyone had been dropped on their head, surely it must have been you."

A titter of amusement from Jamie at this somewhat relieved the tension.

Vera, feeling vastly relieved that her dastardly secret was out in the light of day after all these years – and nobody even believed it – felt a light-headedness which caused her to join in giggling at the absurdity.

Gavin looked at mother and son, and next thing he too joined in the rather hysterical laughter.

Vera knew that all was forgiven when he said: "If you've had a lifelong fear of being dropped on your head, no wonder you wore that ridiculous hat the day I met you ... was it supposed to provide a modicum of protection, in case you should have toppled over the platform at the launching party?"

Vera gave a mock frown. "I thought I asked you never to refer again to that expensive creation from Madame Aimee, it's past history, can't we leave it there?"

He gave her a studied look. "Seems to me, we're casting off quite a bit of family past history, so that's all to the good." Then turning to Jamie he said: "Right then, we'll let you get on your way

96

over to Belmont Terrace to pass on your good news to your grandparents, and, of course, not a word to anyone about that ridiculous little story your dear mother dreamed up. Your Granny Kilgour can worry herself over nothing. If she's looking for a spot of gossip from here, you could, of course, mention that your stepfather is still teasing your mother about her choice of millinery, she'll enjoy that, especially since she had helped choose the monstrosity in the first place. So, be off you, see you soon."

TWO

1897

In the end, a compromise had been reached and with everybody's full agreement, there was to be a more gradual handover of the business, to give Jamie a fair crack at the whip and prove, not least of all to himself that he had the gumption to stick at this career. It had further been decided that the legal formalities of his acquiring the business and the Grosvenor Terrace house would be finalised on his reaching his majority.

At the end of the Gala Evening, celebrating Jamie's twenty-first birthday, Vera turned to Gavin and said: "Thank you, my dear, thank you for everything. And what a happy choice of venue this has been for Jamie's birthday."

Gavin grinned. "Call me an old romantic if you like, but the Grand Hotel will always have a special place in my heart .... it's where I kept proposing marriage to you month after month until you finally agreed. Remember?"

"As if I could ever forget. Mind you, having put up with me for all these years, it's a wonder you ever wanted to set foot in the Grand ever again." They laughed together and headed home for a nightcap, the end of another perfect day in their lives.

The Rich Tapestry of a Tangled Life

1900

As Vera and Gavin came back into the cottage from their walk along the Largs seafront, Vera said: "There now, that wasn't too bad, was it? A good health-giving walk. We should be having that every day and not just when I manage to frogmarch you into it."

Her husband sank back into his favourite armchair, and gave her a baleful look together with saying: "Health-giving, is that what you call it, Vera? Hmph. If I'd known what your idea of my seaside retirement was, I'd have stayed on working in Glasgow."

Vera stopped in the act of removing her long woollen muffler. "Aha, so I was right all along, you do regret handing over all your business concerns to Jamie."

Gavin unfolded his copy of the Daily Record, shook it out to the desired page, and having put on his reading glasses, said: "Vera, you never change, lass, do you? Honestly, you can make a drama out of nothing. And for your information, far from regretting that decision, and in spite of all your horrendous forebodings, I still stand by that decision I made ... and, yes, Jamie is making a success of it and giving us a bit of pocket money into the bargain."

Vera opened her mouth to speak but Gavin was too quick for her.

"Now, having got that out of the way, a hot cup of tea and a toasted scone could be nice. And a bit of peace to read my paper. I want to see how fighting MacDonald is getting on in the latest action against the Boers."

Vera unwound her scarf. "Honestly, men. As long as you've got a comfy chair, your daily newspaper, reports of Britons winning a battle somewhere in the world of our glorious Empire, and a wee wifie to run after you ... then all's well."

Gavin gave a mock frown over the top of his reading glasses. "Couldn't have put it any better myself ... now about that scone?" Vera nodded. "A cup of tea, yes. A toasted scone, no. Until you start getting more exercise, you can forget extra dainty bites. And before this month is over, there'll be a few more morning walks for you, my lad. All too soon it will be the end of October, heading into winter and true to form, if I know you of old, you'll not budge from the fireside."

THREE

As autumn gave way to the biting winds of winter, just as Vera had predicted, her husband got himself comfortably entrenched at the fireside and nothing would move him. After yet another morning of cajoling, persuading and finally a heated argument, still Gavin refused to budge, far less give up so much as an inch of his home comforts.

As Vera was on the point of making a grand exit and leaving him to it, he held out a restraining hand.

"Uch, Vera, listen to me, lass. I worked hard all my days, surely you don't really begrudge me a bit of enjoyment in my well-earned retirement? Surely that isn't too much to ask now, is it?"

"Gavin, surely you know me better than that. It's your health I'm worried about. Look what happened to my father, just months after Jamie's twenty-first, when he gave up business and just lazed around the house all day. My father didn't last long after that massive stroke, now did he? All I'm asking, a bit of exercise, a daily walk and moderation in all things."

Her husband got rather creakily to his feet, led her to a chair and said: "All you had to do was explain your feelings to me, dear. I honestly had not realised that you felt so strongly about this. It's just ..." His words trailed away.

"Just what? If now we're talking frankly, instead of going all around the houses to avoid frank discussion. Let's clear the air once and for all."

"Truth is, Vera, we're just so happy here in this wee cottage, Jamie's still doing well for us with the business ... and ... well, I suppose I have become a bit lazy and complacent. Especially after we solved the problem of what to do about your widowed mother. She is still happy in Millport with Busy Bennet isn't she?"

"And from what you tell me, Gavin, you're happy that's it's just the two of us here enjoying the quiet life. But don't you see, that's the whole point? I want to ensure that it is still the two of us, Darby and Joan, for as long as is humanly possible. Now do you understand?"

He patted her hand. "What I understand is that I'm the luckiest chap on God's earth. So, a daily walk it shall be ... but just don't think you'll get me trailing along as far as the Pencil Monument. After all, as you said, moderation in all things. I suppose that applies to buttered fruit scones as well, does it?"

As the year 1910 opened, Vera found herself reflecting that never before had the twenty-three years age difference between Gavin and herself been quite so apparent.

The Rich Tapestry of a Tangled Life

A very old man, now fast approaching his seventy-seventh birthday, Gavin was gradually becoming more dependent on her as true to his word of yesteryear, he kept up their ritual of a health-giving daily walk along the promenade.

As they approached the cottage, he said: "Do my eyes deceive me, or is that really young Jamie waiting on our doorstep?"

Vera laughed. "Aye, Gavin, it is indeed Jamie, although nowadays as a thirty-four year-old man of business, he hardly merits being called young." Gavin took a firmer grip on his walking stick as he tried to quicken his steps.

"Whatever age he is, he's always a welcome visitor ... albeit a pretty unexpected one on a cold winter's day."

Welcoming greetings over and into the snug warmth of the cottage, the trio settled with cups of tea, slabs of buttered gingerbread and an eagerness to get and exchange family and business news.

Gavin wiped at his rheumy eyes, then looking a his stepson over the top of his reading glasses, the spent old man said: "Jamie, this is indeed a pleasant surprise, after all it's usually springtime before you come to Largs to advise us on the state of business and tell us how we are placed financially. You're doing a grand job, lad, and we're both so proud of you."

Jamie held up a restraining hand. "I beg of you, not another word, there's something I must tell you and I knew I really had to speak to you both in person, a letter in the post ... that would have been too cold, too cruel and much too impersonal."

Gavin frowned, a look of utter bewilderment on his map-lined face, but before he could speak, Vera bent leant forward. "Jamie, whatever it is you've come here to say, out with it. For I've a terrible feeling that it is not going to be good news. Is it Maude? Has something happened to your wife? Or your son?"

Jamie shook his head. "I wish there was some easy way I could tell you this. It's the Bank, the Charing Cross Bank of London, They've posted notices of suspension of business. God help us all."

Gavin breathed out a sigh of relief. "Uch, Jamie, lad, you worry yourself too much, any way, what possible connection can any London Bank have with us up here in Scotland?"

Vera felt the colour drain from her cheeks and in too quiet a voice she asked: "It has nothing to do with us, not so? In any case, given the terrible times we had years ago, with the collapse of the Sillarmore Bank, you've always assured Gavin that his late mother's tried and tested policy of holding on , keeping as firm grip of your own money, unsophisticated or not, that was best."

In the silence that followed, Gavin beamed round in obvious relief.

"Vera, it does credit to your son that he keeps such a close eye on banking matters, even though he steers well clear of banks themselves. Now then, Vera, lass, I think we could all do with a fresh cup of tea."

Vera stared hard at her son. "I somehow think that Jamie has rather more to tell us. And if I'm right, it will be something stronger than tea we'll all be requiring."

Jamie nodded, then raising his head, he spoke: "The Charing Cross Bank of London, it has, or rather had some sixteen Scottish branches, a major one was in Glasgow and ..."

Gavin, broke in. "Even so, still nothing whatsoever to do with us."

Vera rose to her feet then speaking more harshly than she had intended, she yelled: "For God's sake, Gavin, can't you see, don't you yet understand what my son is trying to tell you? He thought he ... an up and coming man of business was too clever for a biscuit tin under the bed ... that was fine for old Lizzie, a street-trailing, bugle-blowing fishwife, but oh no, not for a smart businessman like my son. A bank, that's the place to lodge every halfpenny he owned."

Her son hung his head and mumbled: "But I never thought, after all a reputable Bank and an English one at that, I just cannot understand it."

"Well, if anyone can understand it, it's me," Vera said. "Let us not forget, I've travelled this road before and it was thanks to the Sillarmore's collapse, that you were dropped on your head as a baby."

With a beetroot-red face, Gavin exploded. "Vera, I just cannot believe that you're still going on about that, still propagating that tissue of lies."

FOUR

As she got dressed in readiness to go to her husband's funeral, Vera still felt as though she were living from day to day in a haze of disbelief. And each time she closed her eyes still she could see that scene when as if taking part in some hideous nightmare, she watched in horror as Jamie kneeling down by the side of the old man, he had cradled Gavin's head in his arms. She could despite herself, relive every moment of that terrible day and how Jamie had looked up, all the while shaking his head and broke the news.

"Sorry, Mum, but I'm afraid it would do no good to send for a doctor, your husband has gone."

Then as Jamie had held his mother in his arms and they had wept bitter tears together, suddenly Jamie had drawn away from her as he said: "Mother, arrangements will have to be made. I'll stay here in Largs and help you in every way I possibly can. And while we'll still have financial matters to discuss, this is neither the time nor place. All I will say is that it's a great pity that I never got the chance to finish what I started to tell my stepfather."

Vera wiped the copious tears from her face. "Jamie, I think he heard enough, poor soul, about a bank's collapse."

Jamie nodded. "That was the bad news, Mother, but the good news is that we were not wholly committed to that one bank. I had also made other arrangements. But enough to say at this point, you will never go cold or hungry from poverty, nor will my Maude and my own little family."

Vera's questioning look brought forth the response. "Don't forget Grandpa Kilgour, after his own disaster in the Sillarmore, he taught me well ... put any extra cash into bricks and mortar, my lad. So, all the excess profit went into the bulk buying of large tenement buildings, but we'll discuss all that after the funeral."

The traditional walking funeral as befitted his station was held in Glasgow where Gavin Reid had spent his boyhood, had grown up and had become an important man of business, the string of city shops still bearing his name, witness to the splendid success he had made of his life, having risen from nothing in the way of earthly advantages. He was laid to rest in a plot in the vast Necropolis, adjoining that of his mother, whose grave boasted a large ornate headstone.

Some weeks later in discussing as to which style of headstone, Vera wished to choose for Gavin's grave, Vera put a hand to her mouth, as if deep in thought.

The Rich Tapestry of a Tangled Life

Finally she said: "Although a more modest headstone is not the norm in the grounds of the Necropolis, but that is what I want for Gavin. He never liked anything too showy and given that he did a lot of anonymous charitable deeds, I want money set up in a Trust to be held in readiness to ease the burden of any poverty-stricken victims in any future bank failures. The Sillarmore wasn't the first and I don't suppose this latest one will be the last, and since thanks to your good management, on this occasion, we as a family have not suffered unduly, I feel that Gavin would have felt it only right and proper that we share in some measure our own fortunate escape from such financial ruin."

Jamie put a hand on her shoulder. "I'll get the necessary papers drawn up for us by the Solicitor. And, of course, you're absolutely right about my stepfather not having a taste for anything showy ... remember how for years he went on and on about what he always called your Livadia hat.

Vera laughed. "True enough. And now let that be the last time I ever hear mention of that millinery confection which incidentally cost me a King's ransom from Madam Aimee."

THE END.

Jenny Telfer Chaplin

Also by Jenny Telfer Chaplin:

The Candleriggs Trilogy

Beyond the Bridge of Time

A Life to Live in Glasgow

Published by Bewrite Books

Available as Ebooks from www.Bewrite.net and through Amazon and Barnes& Noble

A Daughter is for Life

Set in Her Ways

Published by Kinnon Enterprises

Available in print from www.Lulu.com and through Amazon and Barnes & Noble.